SIR CH  R

OF

Raul Alcaraz

ISBN
E-book 978-1-7396701-3-9
Paperback 978-1-73967-017-7

Editing, cover art, and book design by PaperTrue Ltd.

Printed in **the United States**

First edition **2022**

Published by: **Paper True Ltd.**

Sir Charlie, Master of the Horse

My name is Charlie, and this is my story.

Everyone, even the doctors, always said I would never amount to anything. You see, I was born unable to use my legs. To everyone else, this meant I was about as useful as a paraplegic racehorse. To make things worse, they said I would always have the mentality of a 10-year-old. I was only about 6 or 7 years old when I heard this, so I thought it was a compliment.

Growing up crippled and stupid (as my daddy would say) was no fun. I mean, I didn't know any better, but as I got older, I realized that some things just didn't seem right.

Mother

She stood outside the local department store, gazing wistfully at a beautiful, long, blue dress she could only dream of having. She closed her eyes and imagined herself wearing it as she walked around town; all the guys looked at her as if she were a princess and all the girls looked upon her beauty with envy.

As she turned away from the window to cross the street, she suddenly felt someone grab her arm, keeping her from going any further. Startled, she turned to see who was bold enough to put a hand on her and heard a voice asking, "Miss, miss, are you ok?" She raised her eyes and saw a tall, handsome man looking at her with concern. He seemed worried about her, probably because she had been standing in front of the shop window for quite some time with her eyes closed.

That was the first time my mother saw Matt, soon to be the love of her life—or so she thought.

They started dating not long after their first encounter. About three dates into their new relationship, she noticed that Matt behaved a bit differently when he drank. She didn't think it was a huge problem at the time; he didn't actually drink too often anyway, so she ignored it as long as she could, until she couldn't anymore.

About a year into their relationship, she was riding the bus back home from work when she started feeling really nauseated. She covered her mouth tightly with her hands, trying hard not to throw up, and waited for the bus to stop. Once it did, she got off in a hurry, then ran as fast as she could around the corner from the stop and let it all out.

She was pregnant, she was sure of it! She was excited but very nervous as well. Matt had already lost a couple of jobs due to his drinking (a pattern that would become all too familiar in the years to come), and she wasn't sure how he'd take the news. He was out "job hunting", so she decided to wait at the dining table to tell him the *good* news when he came home. He finally came through the doors about four hours later. She had fallen asleep at the table, and his entrance startled her awake. His rank breath and staggering gait made it all too clear that he had been drinking. Having had enough, she finally decided to confront him about his drinking. She had a good reason to do it, after all...they had a child on the way!

Saddened, she began to cry, probably knowing deep down that he would never change.

"What's the problem now?" He yelled at her, annoyed. "Don't start with me, I've had a very bad day. No one wants to hire me!"

He tried to hold her and kiss her, but she had had enough. She pushed him away and began to yell at him like she never had. "Why are you doing this, why? I am tired of having to work night and day just to pay the rent and feed us," she continued. "When are you going to change? You have got to stop! It's not just about you and me anymore!"

Just like that, it slipped out. It wasn't exactly how she had imagined telling him. Nevertheless, the cat was out of the bag. He was stunned, at an utter loss for words. She hoped the news would spark some sort of emotion, perhaps compel him to at least *try* to change. But I guess you can't change a person's character. You are who you are till the day you die—at least that's what she believed after that night. Instead of being happy, he actually asked her how she could do that to him. She was ruining his life, his opportunity to BE someone, to DO something! As he ranted at her, she scoffed at him silently. What a joke, she thought to herself.

She tried running to the bedroom, planning to lock the door and cry herself to sleep. But he had other plans. He grabbed her and beat her over and over, aiming a couple of punches to her stomach. Then, he ripped her clothes off and had his way with her. Once he was done, he rolled over on the floor and began to cry. She got up slowly and walked down the dark hallway to her bedroom. An awkward silence filled the house from then on. They did not talk much. An unavoidable mutual need sometimes drew them together at night, but that was that. Their relationship was dead. Her hope that he would change someday into the husband and father she wished he would be slipped away slowly, just like the love she'd once had.

The Ultrasound

The bed was a bit uncomfortable, and so was she as she waited for the doctor. A million emotions swirled through her. Today she would find out if she was having a boy or a girl. She couldn't wait!

The doctor's name was Dr O'Rylee. I would get to know him very well over the years. He had a funny accent. I remember asking him once why he had such a funny voice, and he replied, "Well son, maybe you just have funny ears." That made me laugh. But I'm not sure why he called me son. Was he my real dad?

As the nurse started applying cold gel all over her belly, the doctor asked her where the father was. This made her a bit uncomfortable. The doc realized that he may have overstepped, so he moved on with the ultrasound.

It didn't take longer than a minute to spot that one area that immediately told her she was having a boy. Her emotions got the best of her. She broke down in tears, unable to control herself; it was exactly what she wanted to hear! Soon, however, those tears of happiness would give way to an entirely different emotion.

As the doc continued to perform the ultrasound, he began noticing some very unusual things. The heartbeat was a bit off, and it seemed like only parts of me were moving around in her belly.

Worried, the doc ordered more exams. She caught his unease and immediately asked what was going on, demanding answers in that instant. Unfortunately, the answers would have to wait.

A couple of weeks later, while at work at the restaurant, she got a call from the Doctor's office. The results were in and they needed to talk. She tried to ask over the phone if everything was OK, but they insisted that she come in. This only worried her more. She immediately dropped what she was doing and took off.

There was no easy way to put it. Apparently, she was going to have a baby with serious physical issues, possibly some mental ones too. To try to understand why this happened, the doc asked her if there were any family issues she may have inherited. He also asked about my father (whom he had never met). She knew what had happened though—it was all the physical abuse she had been enduring since she became pregnant. She didn't say anything about it, though; instead, she just told the doc that she wasn't aware of any genetic problems within her family.

In any event, she would have to decide whether to continue with her pregnancy or terminate it. The doc was very straightforward and told her that she was having a baby who would have very special needs; things would not be easy. Once again, she was all alone. In what was once a joyful moment, when she had discovered she was having a boy, when she really needed someone to hold her and tell her that everything would be just fine, even if they had to lie about it…she was all alone.

She looked up at the doc and asked him, "When is our next appointment?" She had decided, almost without a second thought, that she was going to have the baby, no matter what!

And have me she did. For that, I will love momma till the end of time.

Meet My Friends

Because of how I looked and acted, it took me a while to make friends. Let me tell you about the very first friends I did make.

The coffee shop was crowded. Very busy, people everywhere. Some were standing and talking to friends, others were sitting down, reading books or on their computers. A young man, a rocker type, walked over to a young lady in the corner and began to harass her, insisting she give him her phone number. She was obviously annoyed, and was trying to give him the cold shoulder. He put his hand on her arm, saying, "Come on baby girl, let's go somewhere quiet".

She got up and said, "Let go of me, I am not your baby girl!" Just then, her twin sister walked over and looked at the annoying man. She opened her mouth to say something to him, but no words came out. Instead, she just stared at him blankly for what seemed like an eternity. Her seated twin looked at her as if trying to prompt her… they were both panicking. The guy seemed even more confused. And then, someone in the background yelled, "Cut!"

It was a movie set, some kind of low budget production. Everyone let out a sigh of relief as they walked away for a break.

The director was enraged. He walked over to the twins, snapping at the one who had forgotten her lines, "'She isn't your baby girl, but we can both be if you'd like'... that's it! That was your line! What the hell is wrong with the two of you? No one is EVER going to hire either of you! You would have to pay *us* to get you on film! Get out!"

The twins knew they were done but before they walked out, they had a few words for the director. One of them yelled, "We wouldn't work for you if you were the last director on the planet!" The other took her shot by pointing at the fake cup of coffee glued to the table. She lifted the entire table, along with the cup, and yelled, "You think you can afford us? You can't even afford real props, you cheap-ass fucker!" Together they shouted, "We quit!", then stormed off the set with the little bit of dignity they had left.

But things had not always been like this for the twins. Let's go back a few years (quite a few, actually) to when they were about 8 years old...

The stage was set up in the garage. There was stuff everywhere, but the twins somehow made room to drape a blanket over some boxes. They decorated the blanket with some silver glitter and paper stars. They stood in front of their stage and introduced themselves to the make-believe audience.

"Hello, my name is Roxy," said one, taking an awkward bow. The other continued, "And my name is Mariah. Welcome to our show!"

They began acting out all sorts of silly things, mostly improvised, just trying to entertain anyone who would pay attention to them. About 40 minutes later, they looked over at their audience once again and said, "Thank you, thank you very much. We love you!" But there was no one there to acknowledge them—or that's what they thought. As they prepared to take down their stage, they heard enthusiastic clapping, accompanied by a voice yelling, "That was great!"

When they looked over at the corner of the garage, they noticed me sitting just outside it. I had been there from the very beginning, having noticed them by accident. I had been taking a little break from my home-schooling with momma. I was afraid to approach the twins; I didn't really know them, nor did they know me. So I decided just to get as close as possible without drawing attention to myself. I had watched their whole show with great joy. I thought, they had to be professional movie stars to perform so well. So when they finished, I couldn't help myself, and I clapped as hard as I could.

The twins were very surprised, to say the least. They hadn't expected to see anyone there, much less a kid in a wheelchair cheering them on. They looked at each other and smiled, then ran over to me and introduced themselves.

"Hi, my name is Vanessa!" "And my name is Samantha!"

We became friends then. From that day on, I was their number one fan—and, quite honestly, their only one. Every Saturday, the twins put on a show for me, and I watched with even more excitement than the first time; now they were performing just for me!

Then there was Tiny, who scared me a little bit. I mean, he was nice and all, but he was enormous, like a building standing next to me on my race horse (which is what I called my special chair).

Oh, and let's not forget Trey and Chris. They were like brothers, did everything together, didn't go anywhere alone. I wish I had a brother sometimes, so he could stand up for me. Like, literally stand up for me, because I couldn't! It was hard not being able to reach things!

Stephanie

Of all the friends I made, one really meant the world to me...Stephanie. She was the most beautiful girl on the planet, and she was my girlfriend! OK, not really. But if I'd had a good pair of legs, I would have asked her to be my girl.

This is how we met...

I was in my room, when I heard a loud noise outside. Tires screeched, and suddenly there was a loud bang! It took me a minute or so to get on my trusted racehorse. Then, I made my way to the front lawn, which was a task in itself; we didn't have a ramp, so negotiating the front steps was a learned skill. It consisted of building up some speed and leaning way back while literally jumping off the three steps with my eyes closed. I worked up my courage by imagining I was in a race, in the last stretch, which involved a huge tree trunk I had to jump over to cross the finish line.

A fire hydrant had broken, apparently hit by a runaway car. There I was, watching Vanessa, Samantha, Trey, Chris, and Tiny running around and having a blast, soaking themselves under the gushing water. At that moment, I saw her, the most beautiful girl in the world. I wanted to join my friends, but I was afraid they would be too caught up in their fun to see me, or that I would spoil their fun. So, instead, I just imagined myself as the person behind the wheel of the out-of-control car that had hit the hydrant. A little shook-up, I made my way out of the car.

Standing under the water from the hydrant, the beautiful girl walked up to me, held my hand and asked me to dance with her under the magical waterfall. Then, I came back to reality. To my surprise, she was standing right there, in front of me!

She was holding the chair. She asked why I was going back inside the house and if I would like to join her under the "Magical Waterfall," as she called it. I asked her why it was magical, and she said, "Silly, I'm just kidding. It's regular water." I really did feel silly. But right then, I had met my secret love. Most importantly, she was my one and true friend for life.

She introduced herself as Stephanie. I couldn't say anything, so I just sat there with my mouth open. She just smiled and said, "Silly boy, let's go play." So, under the magical waterfall we went.

Later that night, no matter how mean my daddy was to me, all I kept thinking about was how much fun I had had for the first time in my life…and Stephanie's beautiful smile! I know she didn't like me like that, but I dreamed of her every night after that. In those dreams, we were the happiest couple in the world! I had a good strong pair of legs…like tree trunks! And I was the smartest man alive.

All my friends really liked me, and they all knew what I wanted to be when I grew up. You see, I LOVE racehorses! I might not be fast on account of my legs and all, but who would stop me or catch me on a really fast horse? Nobody! I went around telling everybody, "I am Sir Charlie, Master of the Horse!"

I was probably around 10 years old when I saw King Arthur on TV. I was amazed by all the knights in shining armor on their horses. I imagined how cool it would be to have King Arthur walk up to me with his sword and say, "I name you Sir Charlie, Master of the Horse."

For a long time, I had wished daddy would be my King Arthur, I one of his knights, and that I could ride my horse next to him while we went on adventures. The foolish dreams of a child.

Stephanie and Love

"I love you! Will you be my boyfriend?" This is what Stephanie's mother heard as she passed Stephanie's bedroom.

"What the hell? Who is in her room?" She panicked and barged in to see who her daughter was talking to. Stephanie was only about 6 years old at the time, which was even more reason for her mom to panic. When she ran in, she noticed Stephanie holding up a Ken doll to her lips and kissing it. What a relief! Her mother knew she was going to have her hands full as Stephanie got older. "Boys, watch out! My baby girl is going to break your hearts!" She thought to herself.

From a very young age, Stephanie knew she wanted to be in love. She had a kind heart, evidenced by all the strays she kept trying to rescue. She even tried to take in those that didn't need rescuing, like the neighbor's dog! She always saw the good in people too. She attracted friends naturally and effortlessly. Whenever you saw a group of people laughing and having fun, you were bound to see Stephanie right in the middle.

True to her nature, Stephanie fell in love with the very first boy who approached her and asked her to be his girlfriend. Steve.

They dated all the way through high school and got married soon after they graduated. It was all she had dreamed of, to be happily married.

However, not two years after their wedding, they began having problems—serious ones. Steve was spending too much time on his work. He was always away, and Stephanie began feeling neglected (which she was). It's not that he was cheating on her. He just had different priorities. His idea of providing and taking care of her was working his ass off without stopping to actually think about her or what was really important to her.

She tried to talk to him about it several times, but it only started huge fights. Eventually, the inevitable happened. She gave him an ultimatum, which he obviously did not take well, so she filed for divorce. He agreed. Stephanie, the girl who lived for love, took this badly. It was time for her to return home and re-think what really mattered. It would be some time before she found out that love had always existed in her life, even if not the way she imagined it.

Check Yes or No

The most exciting part of my day was when school let out, and Stephanie came by the house for a while to tell me how her day had gone. She also taught me whatever she was learning.

One day, when she came by, she seemed distracted, not like herself. Her thoughts seemed to be somewhere else. I knew that look since I was always "away" on one of my races.

She was holding a note while talking to me. At some point, she put it on the floor to help me turn my chair around, then forgot it there when she left to go back home. I picked it up and went outside to give it back to her, but she was already gone.

Curious, I decided to read it. And this is what it said "Hi Stephanie, would you be my girlfriend? Check yes or no". The note was signed "Steve" at the bottom. I wasn't quite sure what to make of it. I wanted to cry. I was feeling a million different emotions and was confused by them all.

What I did know was that I needed to cross out Steve's name and put my own down! This, somehow, made me feel better. I was calm, and everything was normal. I put the note into the small bag attached to the front of the wheelchair's arm rest and forgot about it.

Back inside the house, my daily verbal beatings were waiting for me. Somehow, as I got older, they seemed to affect me less and less.

The Pizzeria

I didn't go to school, so momma tried to teach me about life and reading and numbers and everything she remembered being taught as a child. It was very hard, however, considering she didn't have the time. She would come home from work for only a little while and rush to her other jobs after making sure I was alright. Of course, she also had to feed my daddy. He would make her really angry—sometimes she needed to leave right away, but he would start a fight because she wasn't spending enough time with him. He always had a bottle of booze in his hand. He kept trying to get her to go to the bedroom with him, which really confused me. I mean, it was daytime. Why did he want to go to bed that early?

As the years went by, my mental condition got a little better. I was able to learn certain things and, with the help of some really nice people from the State, I learned how to integrate into society. I even got myself a job! I was about 22 years old now, and just when I thought only kids could be really mean, I realized that adults were often much meaner.

My very first job! My momma talked to a friend of a friend of a friend who had a friend that worked at the local pizza joint and was able to get me hired. I felt very special since so many "friends" were involved in getting me the job. I wasn't sure what exactly I was supposed to do, but it didn't matter. I showed up on my first day excited and ready to work!

As I struggled to get my racehorse through the front doors, I kept getting in people's way. I felt bad for them; I mean, they just wanted to eat and have a good time with their friends and family, so I kept apologizing. None of them helped me get the door open—instead, they laughed and placed empty pizza boxes on my legs for me to hold, while I actually held the door for them with my chair. I thought I was helping them; it felt good to do something right for someone. Judging by their laughs, they were enjoying my assistance!

Turns out there wasn't much for me to do there. They just had me greet customers and take orders sometimes. Then, one day, Ronnie the pizza maker said he wanted to teach me how to make pizza…man, I was soooo excited!

So, there I was, with Ronnie and a friend of his who was also learning how to make pizza. At first, I was given a large piece of dough and asked to roll it in some flour and toss it up in the air. As I rolled it in the flour, I started to make a mess…flour everywhere! Then, Ronnie's friend started throwing dough and flour at my face. It didn't hurt, but I didn't understand what it had to do with making pizza. Then Ronnie started saying things like, "What a retard! Catch this!" and threw a round piece of dough over my head, covering my face with flour and cheese like he was making a pizza with it. I just sat there, smiling, thinking it must be a fun game. They were both really enjoying it. For several days, I went home covered in different food items. My momma asked me what happened, and I just smiled and told her that I was learning to make pizza. She never thought anything of it.

Stephanie stopped by the pizza joint one day and noticed what was going on. She immediately yelled at Ronnie, telling him to stop it. I wasn't sure why she was so upset, but she grabbed the wheelchair and took me home. She tried telling me that they were making fun of me, and that they didn't care what happened to me. I asked her why they would do that, and she said it was because I was different and they didn't understand me. She said that ignorant people like them do stupid things to good people like me.

Things were different at work from that day on. Ronnie became really mean to me, always yelling at me. As I was going around the counter to greet customers one day, he asked me to help him with something, so I turned around. He was holding some hot marinara sauce and just poured it right on my legs. I didn't feel anything, obviously, and he just yelled, "You see what you did! You stupid retard!"

When I got home later that day, momma asked what happened as she was helping me change. I told her that I had made Ronnie spill some sauce by accident. As she took my pants off, she noticed the burns from the hot sauce on my legs. She started to cry, "Why do you let people do this to you? Why? I'm so tired of this, I can't take it anymore!" It was the first time my momma had yelled at me.

When word got around about what had happened to me at work, Tiny, Stephanie, and the twins were all very upset and mad. I heard Tiny say he was going to kill Ronnie. Everyone told him to just let it be. But, after that night, I didn't see Tiny for a long time. No one told me where he had gone or what had happened to him. I didn't find out until a few years later. Turns out, Brian didn't let things be. He went to the pizza joint and beat Ronnie up so badly he almost killed him. They arrested Brian and gave him a few years for attempted murder or something like that. No one told me, because they didn't want me to feel guilty or bad about it.

Tiny

"Fight, fight, fight!" A bunch of kids formed a circle in the school hall. In the middle, two 6th graders stared each other down. It was like a scene from an old Western. Both cowboys with their hands next to their guns, ready to draw! In this case, though, they were just holding their hands in tight fists, ready to throw the first punch. If you were to take bets on who was going to win, it would have been obvious…Tiny.

Tiny was at least twice the other kid's size, towering over him. You had to give the other poor soul props for not running but, at the same time, you had to wonder what the hell was wrong with him for staying. If they didn't know the story behind the confrontation, one would assume Tiny was being a bully.

Tiny took two steps toward the other kid, wound back his enormous arm, and swung away. At this precise moment, the other kid realized that maybe he should have tried avoiding the fight, or at the very least, he never should have started what he had earlier. He saw Tiny's fist coming at him in slow motion. His eyes got wider as the fist got closer to his chin. There was no stopping it now. Regrets were going to have to wait. It was time to close his eyes and accept what was coming. Sure enough, one hit and the kid went down. If you have ever seen a Rocky movie, then you know what a good knockout punch looks like. Wait…it was more like David and Goliath. No…let's stick to Rocky, I just remembered that Goliath loses that one.

It wasn't longer after the kid hit the ground that the principal reached the spot. The kid was lying on the floor with his eyes closed. The principal looked at Tiny, thinking that Tiny had just killed the kid! "Oh my God, Brian! What have you done?" Before Tiny could say anything, the other kid began to make sounds of pain and agony. After making sure the kid was OK, to the principal grabbed Tiny by the arm and dragged him to his office. Once inside, he kept asking Tiny why had he done that, but Tiny said nothing. He just sat there quietly with a blank expression on his face, almost like there was no remorse or afterthought. The principal gave up and called his mother. Tiny was suspended from that school. It wasn't his first suspension, and it would certainly not be his last.

Tiny's mother was unusually calm as they drove back home. She held his hand the entire way there, as if to let him know she loved him no matter what. It wasn't till they got home that she actually asked him why he had punched the boy. She asked calmly, "My baby boy, what happened this time?" Apparently, he had been in a fight or two before. He looked up at his mom and, with tears in his eyes, replied, "He deserved it mom! He was hitting a girl at recess, and when I found out, I went to him to make him say sorry. He refused and called me an overgrown cow and to mind my own business. That didn't bother me as much as him bullying the girl".

When Tiny's father came home, he found out about what had happened and proceeded to go to his room to discipline him. His mom interfered, though, and tried to calm his father down. Tiny heard his father yelling at his mother, telling her it was her fault, that she was too "soft" with Tiny and he required more "discipline." In Tiny's place, he began to hit her. He pushed her against the wall and held her by the arms tightly as he shook her violently.

Tiny ran out of his room towards his father and started yelling at him. "Let go of my mother, you bully! Let go of her, or I'll beat you up too!"

His father looked down at him and, for a moment, realized what he was doing, what he had been doing all his life. He was abusive toward his wife in front of his son, and Brian could never do anything to defend her. He carried all this anger inside himself. So, whenever he could do something to help someone in need, he did, without thinking about it. This tendency would get Tiny in trouble throughout his life. But he was OK with that. As long as he could, he would be the defender of those who couldn't stand up for themselves...including yours truly.

Bitter Sweet Reunion

As I got older, I noticed that all my friends had gone their own ways toward relationships, jobs, whatever life brought them. They all reached out to me every now and then, but it wasn't the same. I missed them. I missed Stephanie!

Three years after Tiny's incident, he was released from prison. Everyone gathered to welcome him back. We actually all got together at the same pizza joint where it had all started; it was under new ownership now.

Things were going pretty well, and everyone was getting along fine. Then, they started arguing about friendship, and who had been there for me and who hadn't. The twins argued that they had moved away to follow their acting careers. They had only returned when every talent scout and manager told them they sucked and couldn't act to save their own lives.

Trey and Chris had moved to San Francisco to be more "accepted," whatever that meant. But then they decided to come back home and not give a crap about who accepted them and who didn't. They decided to "come out of the closet" that evening. That was weird, because they were never in a closet. I was very confused.

Stephanie didn't say much at first, but when it was her turn, she said a lot. She talked about her failed marriage to Steve. She talked about the fact that I was not her responsibility, that no one there was responsible for me. I could tell that she was hurt, that she didn't mean those things. She was just saying them because she did, in fact, feel responsible for me and like she had let me down. She yelled at Tiny, telling him that everyone had warned him to leave things be that night he attacked Ronnie, and that what he did was his decision. The years he had lost in prison were his doing and no one else's.

Tiny had been drinking heavily and decided he had had enough. He left the party but not before coming to me and getting on his knees, saying, "Buddy, if I had to do it all over again…I would." He walked out, and everyone went their own ways again.

Trey and Chris

From a very young age, Trey and Chris had a very special connection, a bond that just could not be broken. From elementary school all the way to high school, they were inseparable. If Martin Luther King were alive, he would've smiled to see his dream come true (maybe not exactly the way he dreamed it, but still). It was towards the end of their high school years, about the time they were going to graduate, that I heard the twins talking, saying something about them thinking that they were perhaps gay. I didn't know what that meant, at least not at that moment. It wasn't until I accidentally saw what I did that I got a clue.

It was late in the evening, and I had just finished dinner. My dad was yelling at me to make myself useful and take out the trash. Momma was going to do it for me, but dad insisted I do it, saying that I wasn't a complete vegetable and should be able to do simple chores. I looked at momma and smiled while I told her I could do it myself. I then went to the side of the house with the garbage bag on my lap. It was big enough to cover me up completely. I took a moment to catch my breath before attempting to throw it into the garbage can. That's when I saw them.

Trey was holding Chris's hand as he cried. I didn't know what to do. I knew I shouldn't be there, but it was too late to leave. So I sat as quietly and as still as I possibly could. They didn't notice me because of the garbage bag.

Trey was telling Chris, "Let's just get the hell out of this town. No one here will ever accept us, not even our parents!" Chris looked him right in the eye and said, "We will, we'll go somewhere we can just be us and not give a shit about what anyone thinks." For a split second, I thought that maybe people were giving them a hard time because Trey was black and Chris was white. And then they did something I never thought possible between two boys: they kissed each other!

Oh my God! What was I to do? I tried to be subtle, but as I tried to move away slowly, the garbage bag fell on the ground. Oops! Trey and Chris looked over and saw me there, just waving at them in an attempt to break the awkward silence that ensued. They walked over to me. I was soooo scared! I thought it was the end of me. But they hugged me and said, "Don't worry, Charlie. You are our friend, right?" I told them, of course I was because it was true. They asked me to keep what I had seen a secret. To this day, I have never told a single person. No one! They helped me with the trash, and we went on with our lives. Soon after they graduated, true to their promise to each other, they left our little town and it would be years before I saw them again.

San Francisco

Trey and Chris were actually quite successful business partners. They owned a small but quaint coffee shop. Everything they wanted and wished for, they had. Every now and then, they would send me a postcard and pictures of themselves. They never forgot that I was one of their true friends. There was one thing missing from their lives, however. It wasn't all about the money for them. In a way, they missed the small-town life. Time had passed, and certain small town views and opinions had changed. So they decided to pack up and open shop back in their hometown. I would see them again really soon.

Race the Dead

Some time had passed by, as it does, with no regard for anyone and without a pause. Everyone was back on speaking terms, but I still did not see much of them.

It was early in October when I noticed some flyers in the neighborhood promoting a car race on Halloween. The race was called "Race the Dead." This is what I had been waiting for my entire life! A real race I could participate in! The racers were to build their own cars, sort of like a go cart without a motor, and they could make it look like whatever they wanted! So I started building my race car to look like a horse. Every night, I was up till 2 or 3 in the morning, banging my fingers with the hammer and bleeding, but I didn't care. Nothing was going to stop me from entering that race!

I informed all my friends about the race, and they all assured me that they would be there, cheering me on. I couldn't wait to be there with all of them again!

Halloween and the Race

Halloween was here! It was Race the Dead day! My racehorse was ready to go—I had checked it once, twice, hell, a hundred times! I wanted to make sure everything was in place. I just couldn't wait to show everyone what I had always said, how fast I was. My momma helped me into the car and asked if I was ready. I told her it was OK, that my friends were going to be here soon to help me take off. So she stepped back, and hoped and prayed to all the saints she could that I wouldn't be let down. She knew, in her heart, that everyone had forgotten about me. There I was at the start-up line, with racers on both sides, ready to claim victory! There were really young kids with their parents behind them, there were even grandparents with their grandchildren behind them! This was a race for everyone, and let me tell you, *everyone* was there! Well, almost everyone. Turns out there was no one behind me…I was all alone.

Somewhere else, Stephanie, the twins, Trey and Chris, even Tiny, were all getting ready to go to an early themed Halloween party. As they got ready in their own houses, each one began to experience something weird. They all began to feel guilt. Guilt and sadness.

They all had their own memories of growing up together, the fights and the good times. All of it. And in the middle of every memory was yours truly. On this day, all these memories came rushing back like a wild flood, and there was no denying them.

First was Tiny. He began to wonder how alone I probably was, with no one there to stick up for me while he was in prison. He thought, just for a second, how much I probably could have used his friendship had he been around. He kept thinking about the night he beat up Ronnie. Of all the people having regrets, he had the fewest. Nevertheless, he still felt a bit guilty.

The twins were fighting their own battles with guilt. All they could remember was their shows out of their garage and their only true fan, their one true friend who was always there to watch them. Even when they had the big talent show at the high school that I was invited to and everyone said they sucked, I was the one clapping my heart out. I would have given them a standing ovation if I could have.

As they fixed each other's costumes, Trey and Chris started to remember how I could have ratted them out but, instead, they gained a loyal friend who would keep their *secret* for life.

And, of course, Stephanie. As she donned a beautiful white dress with golden flowers all over it, she looked at all the pictures on her dresser. There was one of us in particular that her dad had taken without her knowing, when we were playing in the middle of the street the day she first met me. "That magical waterfall. If only I could go back in time," she thought to herself.

One by one, they continued to get dressed in silence.

Stephanie was all dressed up and looked like a movie star, absolutely stunning! As she went to the garage to get a last-minute prop, she came across my old wheelchair that she had stored for many years. This was the chair I had when I first met her under the magical waterfall. As she stared at it, she noticed a small black bag almost hidden under the arm rest. She reached for it and opened it up.

Inside was my note. It read, "Hi Stephanie, would you be my girlfriend? Check yes or no." It was signed "Steve," but she looked closer and saw where I had crossed out Steve's name and replaced it with my own. Right there, she fell to her knees and began to cry.

Sir Charlie, Master of the Horse

As the start of the race neared, I finally began to realize that no one was coming for me. Only my mother was there, holding back her tears.

It was the first time I actually felt sad and alone and the first time I cried. I lowered my head in defeat and let the tears roll down my face.

Then, out of nowhere, I felt a heavy object on my shoulders and the gentle voice of a giant, "I now name you, Sir Charlie, Master of the Horse." I looked up into the sun, cleaning my tears away, and saw an incredible vision.

Three knights in shining armor and two beautiful ladies of the court stood there. I couldn't believe my eyes. Was I dreaming?

As they drew closer and blocked out the sun completely, I saw who they really were. My friends! ALL OF THEM! Well, almost all of them. Stephanie wasn't there. But I didn't have much time to ask about her. The race was about to start! I sat there speechless; mouth wide open. All five of them got on their knees and vowed to always be there for me. Then they got behind me and pushed as hard as they could!

I felt the wind in my face and basked in the warmth of the sun as I sped down the street. As I got closer to the finish line, I thought I was seeing things. How did momma get there so fast? I got closer and closer and that's when I noticed her…my Stephanie!

She was standing there, waiting for me with the biggest smile on her face. She had tears in her eyes, and I knew what that meant—I missed her too. I was the last to finish the race, but I raised my arms as if I had won! The truth is, I did win, you see. I won the love of my friends! It was the second time I cried, twice in the same day! But this time I cried for joy. The only people that mattered in my life were there. My momma and my friends!

Despite all of the challenges life had thrown my way, I realized that true love and friendship had no boundaries. It didn't matter what your title was (husband, boyfriend, father, whatever). It didn't matter what shade your skin was or who you tried to impress. You just had to be yourself, and eventually your beauty would be seen and appreciated. I love my friends. I love my momma. But mostly, I love my life and I wouldn't change a thing.

I am Sir Charlie, Master of the Horse, and my adventures have only just begun.

Made in the USA
Middletown, DE
24 April 2022

64670710R00024